Excitement at Hollyberry Run

Illustrations by Greg Banning **Text by** Sylvie-Jo

Created by Jeff Tiessen and Randy Rozema

Published by Safe Play Press

Copyright © 1998 by Safe Play Press
132 Main Street East, Suite 1, Grimsby, Ontario, Canada L3M 1P1
ISBN 0-9680667-5-5

Bright sunshine streamed through the windows of Friendly Lodge. Patti Beaver scrambled out of bed, pulling on her fluffy housecoat and furry slippers. She hurried to the window, rubbed her eyes, and gasped with delight!

Patti rushed down the hall to share the good news with her brother and sister. "Wake up, Chip! Wake up, Suzy! This is the day we've been waiting for!"

"Oh look! A fresh new blanket of snow is covering all the hills around Friendly Lodge! After breakfast we can be the first to sail down Hollyberry Run!" said Chip. The eyes of the children sparkled when they saw their favourite tobogganing hill at the foot of Hazy Mountain. "It will be such fun to make fresh tracks through the fluffy snow!" said Patti.

"And look! The maple trees are covered with diamonds! Perhaps Webster, the Watchful Owl, has redecorated his home!" laughed Chip.

Chip, Patti and Suzy chattered happily with their parents at the large oak dining table. "We know you're excited, children, but you'll need a good breakfast to give you energy and keep you warm. It will seem like a long walk up Hollyberry Run!" said Mother Beaver. "Especially pulling your big toboggan!" agreed Father.

The stacks of delicious pancakes, topped with maple syrup, disappeared quickly from their plates. Glasses of milk emptied. The children couldn't wait to get outside!

"Now, remember," cautioned Mother, "Father and I will be watching from here. Stay on Hollyberry Run with Wendy Woodchuck. She is the supervisor on Hollyberry Run, today."

"Yes," said Father, "Hollyberry Run is an ideal slope for you to enjoy. There are no trees or rocks to spoil your fun."

"I'm sure that our guests, the Gopher children, will be joining you before long. And our neighbours, Johnny and Joannie Muskrat, are coming too!" commented Mother.

"Remember to pull your toboggan up the path at the side of the hill," advised Father. "We won't forget!" chimed the Beaver children.

Soon the children were bundled up. They were almost ready to go! "We don't want your scarf hanging out!" said Mother.

"Yes, it might get caught under the toboggan!" agreed Father.

"I'm glad that we have enough helmets at Friendly Lodge for our family and our guests! Everyone uses them for skiing, snowmobiling and skating," said Mother.

"I'm sure the Gopher children will be able to find snugly-fitting helmets, too!" added Chip.

Wendy Woodchuck greeted the children with a smile. "Good morning, children!" she said. "You look ready for some tobogganing fun. Are you ready to go?"

The children made fresh tracks in the snow, pulling their new toboggan up the path to the top of Hollyberry Run. Their friend Webster
the Owl hooted his approval when he saw their warm clothes and pro-
tective helmets. The children would have fun and be safe!

Soon Hollyberry Run echoed with the laughs and shouts of the happy tobogganers. Before long, Johnny and Joannie Muskrat joined the fun.

Wendy Woodchuck helped the children line up their toboggans at the top of the hill. She cheered and waved as she watched them racing down the hill. Just then, Billy and Jenny Gopher came out to play with their new friends, too.

"Hey, Billy! Hollyberry Run is great, but it's not very steep!"

"You're right, Jenny! These other paths look more exciting. I'm sure we could go really fast down this one!"

"Let's go!" Jenny agreed. "Hollyberry Run is fine for the younger kids, but we need a bigger hill!"

Webster's eyes widened in alarm. From his perch, he could see danger. Big rocks were hidden under the blanket of snow. Trees dotted the steep hill leading down to the lake. But the laughter of the excited Gopher children drowned out his warning hoot.

Jenny turned the toboggan toward the steep hill leading right down onto Loon lake. Just then, Wendy and the Beaver children reached the top of Hollyberry Run.

They heard Webster's loud warning, *"Who-who is in danger?"*

"Webster!" called Wendy! "What's wrong?"

"We're having lots of fun," called Chip, "and we're obeying all the safety rules. You don't have to worry!"

But Webster flapped his wings frantically, and called, *"Why-why is there danger?"*

Wendy and the Beaver children knew something was very wrong. "Let's follow Webster!" suggested Chip. "Someone needs help!" As they reached the crest of the hill, they spotted Billy and Jenny. They knew what was wrong.

"Stop, Billy!" yelled Wendy. "Don't go down that path!" shouted Patti.

"Why not?" demanded Billy. "We were just going to try this steeper hill!" explained Jenny. "Webster was trying to warn you. You are in danger!" scolded Chip. "There are trees and hidden rocks on this hill!"

"And, Loon Lake is at the bottom!" added Wendy. "The ice isn't safe for your toboggan!"

Billy and Jenny quickly got off their toboggan, and pulled it back to the top of Hollyberry Run. "Oh!" gasped Billy. "That was too close!" "Thank you Webster!" said Jenny. "And Wendy, we will remember what you taught us. We will stay with you on Hollyberry Run. There are no hidden dangers, there!"

Wendy watched as all the children climbed aboard their toboggans. They glided down Hollyberry Run once more.

Webster, the Watchful Owl, smiled as the hungry children hurried off for lunch. Everyone at Friendly Lodge was safe.

"Help me find a hill that is safe for Chip, Patti and Suzy," asks Webster. Colour the safe hill for Webster.

"How well do you know the safety rules for fun in the snow?" asks Webster. Choose the right answer.

To keep your head safe when you go tobogganing, you should always wear:
a) a baseball cap
b) a feather
c) a helmet

A safe hill for children to go tobogganing has:
a) a clear gentle slope
b) a river or lake or road at the bottom
c) rocks and trees on the hill

Draw a safe toboggan for Chip.
Put yourself on the toboggan wearing a safe helmet and scarf.
Now colour the whole picture.